Vicious Vera

Doggie Tails Series

Vicious Vera

Doggie Tails Series

By David M. Sargent, Jr.

Illustrated by Jeane Lirley Huff

Ozark Publishing, Inc.
P.O. Box 228
Prairie Grove, AR 72753

Cataloging-in-Publication Data

Sargent, David M., 1966–
    Vicious vera / by David M. Sargent, Jr. ;
illustrated by Jeane Lirley Huff.—Prairie
Grove, AR : Ozark Publishing, c2004.
    p. cm. (Doggie tails series)

    SUMMARY: Grandpa plays a trick with
Vera on furniture delivery men.
    ISBN 1-56763-853-8 (hc)
    ISBN 1-56763-854-6 (pbk)

    [1. Lost and found possessions—Fiction.
2. Dogs—Fiction. 3. Stories in rhyme.]
I. Huff, Jeane Lirley, 1946– ill. II. Title.
III. Series.
    PZ8.3.S2355Au 2004
    [E]—dc21   2003091112

Printed in the United States of America

Inspired by

Vera.
The sweetest, most loving, happiest,
most laid-back dog on the planet.

Dedicated to

My friends at Dennis Home Furnishings.

Vera was cuddling
With me on the bed,
When an idea popped
Into Grandpa's head.

An evil plot
He began to contrive,
As the furniture truck
Came down the drive.

"I'm Jack. Is this the right house?"
The driver pried.
"Yes, it is,"
My father sighed.

"Go through the front door
To the room in the back.
But watch out for
The killer dogs, Jack."

"We've locked them up
But they have been trained.
Once they attack,
They cannot be restrained."

"The pups are okay
But the Mama's quite mean.
She's been trained
To be a killing machine."

The men picked up the armoire
And headed on in,
Not knowing the scene
That was about to begin.

While the men worked,
Grandpa snuck 'round
And opened the door
With a leap and a bound.

"The dogs are out!"
He yelled with fear.
"The pups are okay,
But don't let the Mama near!"

The armoire went up
And came down with a crash!
Those delivery men were gone
In a single flash.

They jumped in the truck
And pulled the door down.
They pulled so hard
That the latch came 'round.

The drivers were locked in,
Screaming some sounds—
And wondering if
They would ever be found.

HELP
HELP
KNOCK
KNOCK
BANG
BANG
BANG
GET US
OUT
CALL OFF
the KILLER
DOGS

We finally opened the door,
And there sat the V.
They decided no more furniture
Would be delivered to me.